THE SECRET OF THE
HiDDEN SCROLLS

BOOK THREE
THE GREAT ESCAPE

BY M. J. THOMAS

For Bryan Norman and Peggy Schaefer.
Thank you for believing.

—M.J.T.

ISBN: 978-0-8249-5689-9

WorthyKids
Hachette Book Group
1290 Avenue of the Americas
New York, NY 10104

Text copyright © 2018 by M. J. Thomas
Art copyright © 2018 by Worthy Media, Inc.

Library of Congress Cataloging-in-Publication Data
Names: Thomas, M. J., 1969- author.
Title: The great escape / by M. J. Thomas.
Description: Nashville, Tennessee : WorthyKids/Ideals, [2018] | Series:
   Secret of the hidden scrolls ; book 3 | Summary: "Peter, Mary, and Hank
   journey to the pyramid-studded desert of ancient Egypt. When the trio
   become friends with Pharaoh's daughter, they witness first-hand as Moses
   petitions Pharaoh for the Israelites' freedom. Plagues wreak havoc as the
   group races to decode the scroll, gets chased by a panther, and battles
   Pharaoh's cunning advisor, the Great Magician"— Provided by publisher.
Identifiers: LCCN 2018001359 | ISBN 9780824956899 (paperback)
Subjects: | CYAC: Time travel—Fiction. | Moses (Biblical leader)—Fiction. |
   Plagues of Egypt—Fiction. | Exodus, The—Fiction. | Brothers and
   sisters—Fiction. | Dogs—Fiction. | Egypt—History—Eighteenth dynasty,
   ca. 1570-1320 B.C.—Fiction. | BISAC: JUVENILE FICTION / Religious /
   Christian / Action & Adventure.
Classification: LCC PZ7.1.T4654 Gr 2018 | DDC [Fic]—dc23 LC record
available at https://lccn.loc.gov/2018001359

Cover illustration by Graham Howells
Interior illustrations by Lisa S. Reed
Designed by Georgina Chidlow-Irvin

Lexile® level 46OL

Printed and bound in the U.S.A.
CW
10 9

CONTENTS

PROLOGUE

Nine-year-old Peter and his ten-year-old sister, Mary, stood at the door to the huge, old house and waved as their parents drove away. Peter and Mary and their dog, Hank, would be spending the month with Great-Uncle Solomon.

Peter thought it would be the most boring month ever—until he realized Great-Uncle Solomon was an archaeologist. Great-Uncle Solomon showed them artifacts and treasures and told them stories about his travels around the globe. And then he shared his most amazing discovery of all—the Legend of the Hidden Scrolls! These weren't just dusty old scrolls.

They held secrets—and they would lead to travel through time.

Soon Peter, Mary, and Hank were flung back in time to important moments in the Bible. They witnessed the Creation of the earth. They helped Noah load the animals before the flood. They saw amazing things and had exciting adventures, all while trying to solve the secrets of the scrolls.

Now Peter and Mary are ready for their next adventure . . . as soon as they hear the lion's roar.

The Legend of the Hidden Scrolls

THE SCROLLS CONTAIN THE TRUTH YOU SEEK.
BREAK THE SEAL. UNROLL THE SCROLL.
AND YOU WILL SEE THE PAST UNFOLD.
AMAZING ADVENTURES ARE IN STORE
FOR THOSE WHO FOLLOW THE LION'S ROAR!

1

SOMETHING'S DIFFERENT

Peter stared at the shiny suit of armor standing at the entrance to the hallway leading to Great-Uncle Solomon's library. Something was different. He just couldn't figure out what. Peter slowly reached toward the lion's head on the shield.

"*Ruff!*" Hank barked and tilted his head.

Something was definitely different.

"Mary!" shouted Peter.

"Don't shout," said Mary. "I'm right here."

Peter turned and saw Mary sitting in the comfy leather chair—reading a book, of course.

Mary put her book down. "What are you looking at?"

"Something is weird," said Peter. "But I can't figure it out."

Mary walked over and looked up and down the armor. "The sword."

"What about it?"

"It used to be by his side," said Mary. "Now it is pointing that way."

Peter rubbed his chin. "That's strange." He stepped back. He had always assumed the armor was just armor, but now he wasn't so sure. "I wonder what he's pointing at."

Mary looked in the direction of the sword. "It looks like he's pointing down that hall."

Peter turned. "We haven't explored this one."

Mary walked back to her chair and plopped down. "Have fun. I'm going to finish my book."

"Are you kidding?" said Peter. "A suit of

armor is pointing its sword down a mysterious hallway, and you want to read a book?"

Mary looked up thoughtfully. "Well, maybe it will lead us to another adventure."

Peter grinned and grabbed the big leather bag with the adventure journal inside. "Let's go!"

"*Woof, woof,*" Hank barked and ran down the hall. Peter and Mary were close behind. Hank stopped in front of the third door on the right. He barked.

Peter turned the knob and swung the door wide open. "It's pitch-black in there."

Mary wrinkled her nose. "Gross, what's that smell?"

Peter held his nose. "Maybe it's where Great-Uncle Solomon keeps his dirty socks." He reached through sticky cobwebs and turned on the light.

Mary's jaw dropped. "A sarcophagus!"

"A sarcofa—what?"

"A sarcophagus is a coffin where ancient Egyptians kept mummies," said Mary, like everyone should know.

"Oh." Peter walked over to the colorful stone box. It was covered in jewels and painted with strange winged creatures. It was carved in the shape of a man wearing a blue-and-gold head covering with a snake at the top.

"Another *snake*?" moaned Peter. "Why is there always a snake?"

"A cobra," Mary said. "Ancient Egyptians used it as a symbol of royalty and power. This mummy must have been a ruler or maybe even a pharaoh."

Peter stepped back and bowed. "Nice to meet you, your majesty."

Mary rolled her eyes.

"How do you know so much about mummies?" said Peter.

"I read about it in a book," said Mary. "It was called *Are You My Mummy?: A Look Inside Ancient Pyramids.*"

Peter ran his hand across the top of the sarcophagus. "Let's open it."

"I don't think we should," said Mary, backing away.

"You're afraid of mummies!" said Peter.

"No, I'm not," said Mary.

Peter grabbed one end of the lid. "Then help me open it."

Mary slowly reached for the other side.

"I wouldn't do that," said a raspy old voice from behind them.

Peter jumped. He turned to see Great-Uncle Solomon walking in the doorway. Great-Uncle Solomon brushed cobwebs out of his bushy white hair and glanced around. "I really need to clean in here," he said.

"Why can't we open it?" said Peter. "Will the mummy escape?"

Great-Uncle Solomon laughed. "No, that's only in the movies."

Mary folded her arms and gave Peter a look like he should have known that.

"That mummy has been dead for thousands of years," said Great-Uncle Solomon. "I don't think you'll like how he smells."

Hank sniffed the sarcophagus and jumped back.

Great-Uncle Solomon held out two apples. "Here, I brought you a snack."

Peter shoved them into the big leather bag. "Thanks, I'll save them for later."

"I can't believe you're not hungry," said Mary. "You're always hungry."

Peter pinched his nose. "The smell ruined my appetite."

"Take a look around the room," said Great-Uncle Solomon. "It's filled with treasures and artifacts from my explorations in Egypt. You might even find something to help on your next adventure."

Peter walked over to a shelf and picked up a

dagger with jewels on the handle. He slipped it in his bag.

Mary unrolled a scroll and her eyes lit up. "Maybe we should take this map."

Peter stuck it in the bag.

Roar! A lion's roar echoed through the house.

Great-Uncle Solomon grabbed a flashlight and some binoculars and handed them to Peter. "Every good explorer needs these."

Roar!

"Let's go!" said Peter. He hung the bag over his shoulder, ran down the hallway, and passed the suit of armor. Mary and Hank were right on his heels. They skidded to a stop at the library doors. Peter reached for the lion's-head handle and turned.

Click!

Peter swung the door open, and they ran into the library.

Mary shuffled through the books and pulled out the red one with a lion's head painted in gold on the cover. The bookshelf rumbled and slid open to reveal the secret room. It was dark except for the glowing clay pot in the center that held the hidden scrolls.

Mary ran over to the pot. "I want to pick the scroll this time."

"Be my guest," said Peter.

Mary closed her eyes and grabbed one.

"What's on the red wax seal?" said Peter.

Mary squinted. "It looks like a triangle."

"Let's see where it takes us," said Peter.

Mary broke the seal. Suddenly, the walls shook, the floor quaked, and books flew off the shelves.

Peter grabbed Mary's hand. "Here we go!"

The library crumbled around them. Then everything was still, quiet, and hot—very hot.

2

THE GOLDEN DOOR

"It's so hot!" said Peter.

Mary shaded her eyes with her hands. "The sun is really bright."

Peter spun around. "There is nothing here but sand."

"We must be in the middle of the desert," said Mary.

"We just got here and I'm already thirsty," said Peter.

"Did you pack any water?"

"No," said Peter. "We only have the apples."

Mary wiped sweat from her forehead. "Let's find some water."

"*Ruff!*" Hank barked and took off, kicking up sand behind him. He ran to the top of a sand dune and spun in circles, barking.

"Did you find water?" Peter shouted. He climbed up the tall sand dune. "Mary, come look."

Peter tapped his foot as Mary slowly climbed the dune. He couldn't believe how slow she was, especially with all of her karate training.

Mary finally reached the top and took a deep breath. "What is it?"

Peter pointed at a tall pyramid in the distance. "I think I found Egypt."

Mary's eyes widened. "I've always wanted to go to Egypt. I can't believe I'm actually here."

"Let's go!" said Peter.

Mary took off running toward the pyramid. She beat Peter and Hank there.

"I didn't know you could run so fast," said Peter.

"Let's explore," said Mary.

"How do we get in?" said Peter. "Did any of your books tell you?"

"There should be an entrance," she said. "But I don't see one."

Hank sniffed along the base of the pyramid. He started digging, flinging sand everywhere. Peter joined him and found a tiny entrance in the rock. He bent down and squeezed through. Mary and Hank followed.

Mary stood up and brushed off the sand. "It's dark in here."

Peter unzipped the leather bag and pulled out the flashlight. "Let there be light," he said, shining the beam down a long hallway. The floors and walls were made of large stones covered in paintings of people and strange animals. Some of the people were working and some were sitting on thrones.

"Look," said Mary. "I see some light."

They ran to the end of the hall and turned the corner to see another long hallway with torches lighting the way. Mary grabbed one.

Hank ran in front of them and barked. Peter followed closely behind him. Around the next corner, they found a tall golden door. It had a painting of a big black cat with wings. Hank froze and growled at the cat. Peter reached to open the door.

"Stop," said Mary. "I don't think we should go in there."

"Why not?" said Peter. "Are you afraid of mummies?"

Mary stepped back from the door and lowered her head. "Maybe a little," she admitted.

"You don't need to be afraid," he said. "Hank and I are here." Peter stood tall and pulled his shoulders back.

Hank barked and wagged his tail.

"Remember," Peter said. "God will help us."

"You're right," said Mary. "Let's do it."

Peter pushed against the massive door, and it creaked open to reveal a dark room. Peter could feel Mary and Hank crowding close to him as they all crept in. He swept his flashlight around the cavernous space. Paintings covered the walls all the way up to the high ceiling—which had a large eyeball painted in its center. Peter felt like it was looking at him.

Mary walked around the room with her

torch. "This is amazing. Look at all of these treasures!"

The light of Peter's flashlight glittered on jewel-covered vases and statues.

Hank barked at something in the center of the room.

Peter followed Hank's bark with his light. "Look, Mary!" he shouted. "A sarcophagus."

"It looks just like the one Great-Uncle Solomon found!" said Mary. She looked around again. "This room must be a tomb." She shivered.

"Let's open it," said Peter. He grabbed the lid, but it wouldn't budge. He unzipped the leather bag and pulled out the dagger.

"Be careful," said Mary.

Peter slid the dagger into a crack under the lid.

Pop. The lid moved. Peter and Mary slid it open and looked inside. There was a mummy wrapped in white cloth.

"Yikes!" Peter stepped back, then he leaned forward. "Hey, it smells like cinnamon." He put the dagger back in the bag.

"Let's put the lid back on," said Peter. "I'm getting a strange feeling."

"Me too," said Mary. "Maybe we shouldn't have opened it." She helped him slide the lid back in place.

Hank turned away and growled.

"What is it?" said Peter. He shined the flashlight into the corner. A pair of glowing yellow eyes shined back at him. Peter saw the shape of a huge black panther. "Don't worry, Hank. It's just a statue."

Roar! The panther leaped on top of the sarcophagus.

"It's alive!" shouted Peter. "Let's get out of here!"

3

THE BLACK PANTHER

Peter, Mary, and Hank ran out of the tomb. Peter slammed the door shut. He could hear the panther's claws scraping on the door and stone floors.

They ran down the hallways and found the entrance to the pyramid.

"Hurry," said Peter. "That door won't hold it for long!"

Mary and Hank squeezed out through the opening. Peter shined the light down the hallway. The glowing yellow eyes were moving quickly toward him. Peter dropped the flashlight and dove through the hole.

The panther tried to follow, but it got stuck in the opening. It clawed at the sand, fangs flashing.

"Run!" shouted Peter.

They ran across the hot sand toward a wide, rushing river. Peter paused at the riverbank and looked back. The panther was free!

"Jump in!" shouted Mary, as she dove into the cool water.

Peter and Hank jumped in after her. The current swept them to safety. The panther paced angrily on the bank, but it didn't get in the water.

The river carried them away from the pyramid and the panther. At a bend in the river, they all got tangled in the tall grass along the riverbank.

Peter struggled to stand as the current rushed against him. "I can't get out!"

A hand reached through the thick grass. "Grab

my hand!" said a girl's voice.

Peter grabbed the hand and held tight. He stepped onto the muddy riverbank.

The girl looked about the same age as Mary. She wore a white dress with a golden belt. Her necklace was thick gold covered in red rubies and green emeralds. A colorful headband held back her dark hair. She was very pretty—not that Peter noticed.

"You're strong," said Peter.

"Thanks," said the girl. "And you're wet."

The grass rustled behind Peter.

"Hello!" shouted Mary. "Can somebody please help me?"

"Oh, yeah," said Peter. "I almost forgot." He reached down and pulled Mary out of the water.

"Thanks." Mary gave Peter a look. "What ever happened to 'Girls go first'?"

Peter shrugged. "Sorry. She grabbed my hand first."

"My name is Shephara," said the girl.

"I'm Peter," he said. "This is my sister, Mary."

Peter set his bag under a palm tree and unzipped it. Everything inside looked dry, including the scroll. Peter sighed in relief. If the scroll got wet, they would be in big trouble.

"*Ruff!*" Hank crawled out of the river. He shook, and water sprayed everywhere.

"Hank, stop that!" said Peter. "Don't get Shephara wet."

Shephara wiped her face. "It's okay." She petted Hank's head. "Where did you find this beautiful creature? I have never seen a dog like him."

Hank walked around with a spring in his step.

"We brought him from home," said Peter.

"Where are you from?" said Shephara. She looked Peter up and down. "You don't look like you're from around here."

Mary gave Peter a look that said, *Don't answer that*. "We came from far away," said Mary.

"Are you from Nubia?" said Shephara.

"No," said Mary, "much farther."

"Then you must be tired from your long journey," said Shephara.

"Yes," said Peter. "And hungry."

Shephara's eyes brightened. "You can stay with my family. We have dry clothes and food."

Peter rubbed his belly. "Sounds good to me. Let me grab my—" Peter turned and saw a camel with its head stuck in the bag. The camel was chewing the last bites of the apples.

"Oh, no," said Peter. "That was all of our food."

The camel stuck its head back in the bag and pulled out the scroll.

"No!" Peter ran over and grabbed it out of the camel's slobbery mouth. The camel lifted its long neck and curled its lips.

"Watch out, Peter!" shouted Mary.

It was too late. Spit flew out of the camel's mouth, right at Peter.

"Ugh, gross!" grunted Peter, wiping the mess from his face.

Mary and Shephara laughed so hard they could barely stand.

"Now I *really* need to change clothes," said Peter.

Shephara tried to stop laughing. She climbed up onto the camel's humped back. Another camel walked up and bumped into Peter. "Would you like a ride to my house?"

Peter shook his head. "No, thanks! I'll walk."

Mary climbed up onto the other camel. "I've always wanted to ride one."

"Where's your house?" said Peter.

"We just follow the Nile River," said Shephara. "It's not far."

They walked and rode alongside the river. The farther they traveled, the more activity they saw. Boats with fishermen filled the water. Square houses made of large mud bricks lined the river.

People picked vegetables and fruits in small gardens. No matter what they were doing, the people all stopped and bowed as Peter, Mary, Shephara, and Hank passed.

"Why is everyone bowing?" asked Peter.

Shephara just giggled. "We're almost there."

As they rounded a bend in the river, Peter saw a huge palace. A large stone porch went to the edge of the river. Tall white columns held up a pyramid-shaped roof.

"We're here," said Shephara.

Five large men with spears rushed out and helped Shephara down from her camel.

Mary hopped off and joined Peter and Hank. They walked toward Shephara.

The guards rushed over and surrounded Peter, Mary, and Hank, pointing long, sharp spears at them. "Step back from the princess!" shouted the guard who was obviously in charge.

4

So Many Snakes

"*Princess?*" exclaimed Peter, his eyes wide.

"You are under arrest!" the guard shouted.

"Let them go, Captain!" said Princess Shephara. "They're with me."

"Yes, Princess," said the Captain. "As you wish." The guards put their spears down and backed away.

Peter let out a deep breath. He turned to Shephara. *A princess!* He had never been around royalty before. Peter bowed awkwardly. "Um, it's nice to meet you, your Highness."

Princess Shephara giggled again. "You don't have to call me that."

Mary gulped. "What should we call you?"

"Just call me Shephara," she said. "We're friends."

The guards took their places at the entrance of the palace.

"Let's go inside and get out of this heat," said Princess Shephara.

The Captain narrowed his eyes and stared at Peter.

"I'm with her," said Peter. He pulled the leather bag closer to his side and quickly walked past the guard.

Princess Shephara turned and stretched her arms wide. "Welcome to my home!"

Peter looked around the huge palace. Tall pillars held up a high ceiling painted with stars and a moon, and colorful carpets covered the smooth stone floor. Statues of sphinxes guarded a grand staircase that led to large golden doors.

Hank growled at one of the sphinxes. It had the body of a lion and the head of a man.

"It's okay, Hank," said Peter. "It's not alive."

Hank kept growling.

Peter pointed up the stairs. "What's up there?"

"My dad," said Shephara. "You can meet him later."

A shiver went through Peter. If Shephara was the princess, her dad must be . . . the king? He wasn't sure about meeting such an important person.

Shephara clapped her hands twice. "Slaves!" she shouted. "Come!"

Men, women, and children ran to Princess Shephara from all sides. They all wore white skirts—even the men and boys. One of the boys waved a fan of colorful feathers. Peter noticed that the slaves looked different than the Egyptians.

"These are my friends," said Princess Shephara, gesturing toward Peter and Mary. "Dress them in our finest clothes."

Peter looked at Mary. She opened her mouth, as if she were about to say something, then closed it. Peter's stomach growled loudly.

Princess Shephara looked at Peter. "And they need food," she said. "Lots of food."

"Yes, Princess," said one of the slaves. "As you wish."

A skinny young boy crept up to Peter. "Come with me, sir."

Peter felt weird being called *sir*. He followed the boy to another room. The slave laid a white wraparound skirt, a colorful belt, and leather sandals on a soft chair in the corner.

"Thanks," said Peter.

The slave wouldn't look at Peter.

"My name is Peter."

The boy slowly looked up. "My name is Joseph."

Peter tilted his head. "That doesn't sound like an Egyptian name."

"It's not," Joseph said. "My people are Israelites, and I'm named after my great-great-great-grandfather. He was a ruler here, but that was four hundred years ago." He lowered his head again. "Now we are slaves."

Peter felt awkward. He had never met a slave before. "Is it awful being a slave?"

Joseph slowly nodded his head. "I never get

to do anything I want to do. All I do is work."

"Where are your parents?" said Peter.

"They are slaves too," said Joseph. "They have to work even harder than I do." He walked over to the window and pointed across the river. "They work all day in the hot sun making bricks."

Peter felt bad for Joseph and his family. "That sounds terrible. Can't anybody help you?"

"No," said Joseph. "There is no one to help us. We just want to be free."

Peter was about to say something when a loud bell rang throughout the palace.

"The feast is ready," said Joseph. He scurried off with his head down.

Peter put on his new Egyptian clothes and made a face. He had never worn anything like this before, but Shephara did say they were the finest clothes in Egypt. He picked up the bag and made sure the scroll was hidden deep inside. He and Mary would have to look at the scroll soon. He held the bag tightly and made his way to the feast.

Mary was dressed a lot like Princess Shephara. Peter almost didn't recognize her. Hank was wearing a golden collar covered in jewels.

Mary pointed at Peter and laughed. "You're wearing a skirt!"

"It's not a skirt," said Peter in his deepest voice. "It's some kind of ancient kilt."

Princess Shephara joined them. "Your skirt looks great, Peter!"

Peter folded his arms. "It's not a skirt!" He was glad his friends at home couldn't see him.

"The feast is ready," said Shephara.

They followed Shephara into a room filled with colorful rugs and tables surrounded by pillows.

Peter plopped down on one of the comfy pillows. Mary lowered herself gracefully.

Princess Shephara clapped her hands three times. "Let the feast begin!"

Slaves came from everywhere, offering trays overflowing with food. Peter's mouth watered. He loaded his plate with warm bread, sizzling fish, and cake covered in honey. He grabbed some grapes and leaned back on his pillow. "Egyptians sure do know how to eat."

Mary filled her plate with lettuce, cucumbers, and carrots.

Peter rolled his eyes. "You're going to eat a *salad* with all this delicious food?"

"I like salads. They're healthy," said Mary, sounding like their mom.

Hank slurped some mashed-up mess out of a

big bowl. Peter didn't know what it was, but Hank loved it.

A slave picked up a mallet and banged a gigantic gong. The ring echoed through the room and everyone froze. The doors swung open and a tall man walked in wearing a white skirt with golden tassels. He wore a blue-and-gold head covering with a jeweled cobra in the center. He held a tall stick in his hand with a hook on the top. It looked like a shepherd's staff.

He walked straight toward Peter, Mary, and Shephara.

"This is my dad," said Shephara, "Pharaoh."

Peter got a lump in his throat. "Nice to meet you, your Pharaohness . . . um, I mean, your majesty."

"You can just call him Pharaoh."

Peter looked at Mary. She stood frozen. "Mary is pleased to meet you too," he said.

Mary blinked, but she still didn't move.

"Welcome to my palace," said Pharaoh. "The slaves will take care of anything you need."

The Captain rushed in and whispered something in Pharaoh's ear.

"I have visitors," said Pharaoh. He turned and walked away.

More guards joined him as he left the feast. The Captain frowned at Peter as he walked out.

"Let's follow," said Shephara. "This could be interesting."

"I don't know," said Peter. "The Captain doesn't seem to like me."

"He doesn't like anyone," said Shephara. "Just be quiet and stay close to me. You'll be safe."

The trio followed Pharaoh and the guards out to the porch beside the Nile River. They hid behind a pillar.

"Bring the visitors," said Pharaoh.

Peter peeked around the pillar. He saw two men with long gray beards in dusty robes.

"My name is Aaron," said one visitor. "And this is my brother Moses. We are here to deliver a message."

"What is it?" asked Pharaoh.

Aaron cleared his throat. "God says, 'Let my people go!'"

Peter wondered what people he was talking about.

Pharaoh laughed. "I don't know your God," he said. "And I will not let them go!"

Moses stepped forward. "The God of Israel said to let his people go!"

Peter realized the men were talking about the Israelites—the slaves like Joseph.

The guards rushed to protect Pharaoh and drew their swords.

Pharaoh waved his hands and the men stepped

back. "If your God is so powerful,
show me a miracle."

Moses turned to Aaron and said,
"Throw down your staff."

Aaron threw his staff to the ground. It turned
into a big, slithery snake.

Pharaoh jumped back. "Nice trick." He clapped
his hands. "Bring my magicians!"

A guard ran into the palace and returned with several men in long robes. One, wearing a purple robe, walked to the front and bowed to Pharaoh.

"How can I help you?" said the magician in purple.

"That man turned his staff into a snake," said Pharaoh.

Peter leaned out to see what was going to happen.

The magician in purple turned suddenly and looked into Peter's eyes. His lips formed an evil grin.

"Snakes are my specialty," the man said. He threw down his staff, and it turned into a colorful snake.

Then the other magicians threw down their staffs, and the staffs turned into snakes.

Peter backed farther away and groaned. "Oh, why do there *always* have to be snakes!"

5

TROUBLE IN EGYPT

Snakes slithered everywhere!

"Grrrr!" Hank growled at one that was making its way around the pillar toward them.

The snake rose up and was face-to-face with Princess Shephara. Its forked tongue flicked between sharp fangs. Shephara stepped back.

Mary spun and kicked the snake in the side of the head. It fell to the floor with a thud. Then it slithered away and joined the other snakes.

"Thanks," said Princess Shephara. "That was close."

"You're welcome," said Mary.

Peter looked back toward the men. The magicians' snakes circled around Aaron's snake, hissing and poised to attack.

Then Aaron's snake coiled up and darted at each of the others. It swallowed every other snake.

Pharaoh glared at the magicians. They hung their heads and slowly walked away. Moses reached down and picked up the snake by the tail. It stiffened and transformed back into the staff.

"Is it just me," Peter murmured to Mary, "or does the staff look a little bigger?"

Moses pointed the staff toward Pharaoh. "Now will you let the people go?"

"No!" said Pharaoh. "Guards, take them away!"

The guards surrounded Moses and Aaron and led them away from the palace.

Princes Shephara tapped Peter on the shoulder and whispered, "Let's get out of here before my dad sees us."

They ran back into the palace.

"That was close," said Princes Shephara.

"I think the magician in purple saw me," said Peter.

"Oh, no!" said Princess Shephara. "He tells my dad everything."

"Who is he?" said Mary.

"He's the Great Magician," said Shephara. "He has great powers. My dad listens to all he says."

Princess Shephara led Peter, Mary, and Hank to the other side of the palace. Slaves bowed to the princess along the way. Peter glanced at Mary. She looked as bothered by this as he was.

"Why won't your dad let them go?" she finally blurted out.

"He's stubborn," said Shephara, frowning. She stopped and pointed at a door. "Here's your room," she said. "Make yourselves at home. I'll see you in the morning."

They entered a large room with three beds. Even Hank had his own bed. Peter closed the door and pulled out the scroll.

"Let's see what it says," said Mary. "We won't have much time to solve it."

Peter unrolled it on a table in the corner of the room. "It looks like the symbols and pictures we saw on the walls of the pyramid."

Mary took a closer look. "It's hieroglyphics . . . just like in the pyramid."

Peter grinned. "I was right."

Whoosh! A gust of wind blew through the window and almost blew the scroll off of the table. Michael the angel flew in with his mighty wings spread wide.

"I'm glad to see you," said Mary. "It's been an interesting afternoon."

Michael looked at Peter and Mary. "I have some serious things to tell you."

Mary's eyes got big. "What?" Mary liked serious things.

"The Egyptians have a very good life . . . especially Pharaoh," said Michael. "But life in Egypt is about to change."

"Why?" asked Peter.

"Pharaoh and the Egyptians have been very mean to the Israelites," said Michael. He pointed out the window toward the slaves, who were still working on the other side of the river. "They turned them into slaves, and they force them to work very hard. They even treat the Israelite children badly."

Peter frowned. Joseph was one of those children.

Michael pointed to the sky. "God has heard the Israelites' cries for help, and he is not going to let them be abused any longer!"

"What's going to happen?" said Mary.

"You will have to wait and see," said Michael. "Now let's go over the rules for your adventure."

Michael held up one finger. "First rule: you have to solve the secret of the scroll in fourteen days, or you will be stuck here."

Peter wrinkled his forehead. "Why do we have fourteen days instead of seven days?"

"This adventure is going to take a little longer," said Michael. "Pharaoh is very stubborn."

Hank's ears perked up. He looked at the door and growled. They all got very quiet, and Michael disappeared. Peter peeked out the door and saw guards walking down the hallway.

"They're gone," he said and gently closed the door.

Michael reappeared. "I need to hurry in case they come back." Michael held up two fingers. "Second rule: you can't tell anyone you are from the future."

Michael handed Peter the flashlight. "I think you dropped this at the pyramid."

"Oops," said Peter.

"Hide it," said Michael.

Peter shoved the flashlight in his bag.

"Wait," said Mary. "You saw us there?"

"Yes," said Michael. He held up three fingers. "Third rule: you can't try to change the past."

Hank's ears perked up again. He crept toward the door.

Michael spread his wings. "I must go."

"Don't leave yet," said Mary.

"Keep your eyes open for Satan, the enemy," said Michael. "He is causing a lot of trouble in Egypt and deceiving many people."

"*Grrr!*" Hank growled at the door.

Bang! Bang!

Mary looked at the door. "Should we answer?"

"Be careful," said Michael. "Terrible things are coming!" Michael spread his wings and shot out of the window like a lightning bolt.

Bang! Bang!

"What do we do?" said Mary.

6

THE GREAT MAGICIAN

Bang! Bang!

Mary walked toward the door.

"Wait!" whispered Peter. He ran over to the table, rolled up the scroll, and hid it in the leather bag. Then he threw the bag on the bed and sat on it. "Okay, let them in."

Mary swung the door open.

The Captain looked around suspiciously. "What's going on in here?"

"Nothing," said Peter. "We're just getting ready for bed."

The Captain looked behind the curtain. "I thought I heard a man's voice."

"Maybe you heard me," Peter said in his deepest voice.

"No, it was a man's voice," said the Captain.

Hank growled as the guard knelt down and looked under the beds.

"Maybe it was Hank," said Peter. "His growl is pretty deep."

The Captain kept looking around. "There's something fishy going on here."

Sweat popped out on Peter's forehead. "Nothing fishy going on here," he said. "Maybe you're smelling the Nile River."

"I don't trust you kids," said the Captain.

Hank growled again.

"Or your dog," said the Captain. "I'll be watching you."

"Good to know," said Peter. "Makes me feel safe."

The Captain left and Mary shut the door.

"That was close," said Peter. He unrolled the scroll on the table and looked at Mary. "Have you read any books about hieroglyphics?"

"A few," said Mary. "I can tell there are eight words by the way the symbols are arranged. But I don't recognize the symbols."

Peter pointed at the first symbol. "That one looks like a flag," he said.

"Is the first word *flag*?" said Mary.

They waited. Nothing happened to the scroll.

"This might be harder than I thought," said Mary.

Peter grabbed the adventure journal and sat on his bed. "You keep trying to solve the secret of the scroll," he said. "I've got a couple of things to write down."

Day 1

Egypt is awesome but very hot! I'm not a fan of camels. I could get used to living in the palace if it weren't for the slaves. The Egyptians treat them so badly. Princess Shephara seems pretty nice. But I'm worried about Michael's warning that terrible things are coming.

Peter, Mary, and Hank climbed into their beds. A breeze blew the cool night air through the window as they drifted off to sleep.

The morning sun reached Peter's eyes, and he sat up in bed.

Mary was already awake and looking at the scroll.

Peter looked over her shoulder. "Have you figured it out yet?"

Knock-knock!

"Hide it!" whispered Mary.

Peter put the scroll in the bag and hid it under the bed.

"Who is it?" he asked.

"It's Joseph."

Mary opened the door.

"Princess Shephara requests that you meet her down at the Nile River," said Joseph.

Peter looked out the window and saw Princess Shephara swimming.

"Can you come with us?" said Peter.

"No, I can't," said Joseph.

"Why not?" said Mary.

"I have work to do. I'm not allowed to play," said Joseph. He lowered his head and walked out of the room.

"Hurry!" Princess Shephara's voice floated through the window.

"We don't want to keep the princess waiting," said Peter.

They ran down to the river.

Princess Shephara splashed water on Peter. "Get in! The water's perfect."

Peter and Mary jumped in and swam over to Princess Shephara. They splashed and played in the Nile like it was a swimming pool back home. Peter looked up at the palace and saw Pharaoh and the magicians walking down to the river.

"Good morning, Dad," said Princess Shephara.

"Good morning," said Pharaoh. He looked out. "My kingdom looks amazing this morning!"

Peter looked out and saw Moses and Aaron walking beside the river.

"Look who's back," said the Great Magician with an evil stare.

Moses and Aaron drew closer. Moses stepped forward. "The Lord, the God of the Hebrews, has sent me to tell you to let his people go!"

"No," said Pharaoh. "I will not let them go."

Moses replied, "Then God has a message for you. He says, 'I will show you that I am God!'"

Moses turned to Aaron and said, "Raise your staff and strike the Nile River!"

Mary's eyes widened. "Get out of the water!"

"Why?" said Princess Shephara.

"Trust me," said Mary.

Peter, Mary, and Shephara quickly swam toward the riverbank.

Aaron swung his staff and hit the surface of the water. A red circle appeared at the spot he hit.

It grew bigger and bigger.

"Hurry," said Peter.

The dark circle filled the Nile River. Peter scrambled out just before the circle reached them.

"What is it?" said Princess Shephara.

"It looks like blood," said Mary.

"Gross!" Shephara shuddered.

Dead fish floated to the top of the river, and a strange stink filled the air.

The Great Magician slowly clapped his hands. "Nice little trick." He grabbed a pitcher of water and poured it on the ground. He held his staff above his head and stuck it into the puddle. He mumbled some words Peter couldn't understand. A red circle came from the bottom of the staff and filled the water.

Pharaoh stuck his finger in the puddle and smelled it. "Blood," he said.

Pharaoh and the magicians turned and strolled into the palace like nothing had happened. Moses and Aaron shook their heads and walked away. The water was red for as far as Peter could see.

"That didn't go well," he said.

"Why won't your dad listen to Moses?" Mary said.

"He is *very* stubborn," said Princess Shephara.

"He seems to listen to the magician in the purple robe," said Mary.

Princess Shephara lowered her head and sighed. "He spends more time with the Great Magician than with me."

"How long has he been helping your dad?" said Peter.

"For a long, long time," said Princess Shephara. "The Great Magician was around before my dad was Pharaoh."

"He makes my skin crawl," said Peter.

7

Frogs, Frogs Everywhere

Peter woke the next morning to the sound of barking outside the window. He looked out and saw Mary and Hank playing with Shephara. He grabbed the bag and ran out to join them.

"Princess Shephara!" the Great Magician shouted from the palace. "It's time for school!"

Peter shrugged. "I guess playtime is over."

"He's your teacher?" asked Mary.

"Yes," said Shephara. "I can't go to school, so he comes to the palace."

"Why can't you go to school?" said Mary.

"Because I'm a girl," said Shephara.

Mary put her hands on her hips. "Well, that's not fair."

"Rules are rules," said Shephara.

"But you're the princess," said Peter. "Can't you change the rules?"

"Only the Pharaoh can change the rules."

"Maybe you will be Pharaoh someday," said Mary.

"If I become Pharaoh," said Princess Shephara, "I will change a lot of rules."

"School is starting!" shouted the Great Magician.

"We better go," said Princess Shephara. "The Great Magician doesn't like it when I'm late."

"What's he going to do?" said Peter. "Turn you into a frog?"

Princess Shephara knelt down and hopped. *"Ribbit, Ribbit."*

"Right this way, Princess Frog," he said.

They all hopped to class—even Hank.

As they walked into the classroom, Hank growled at the Great Magician.

The Great Magician pointed at small tables lined up in the middle of the classroom. "Have a seat. Today, I will teach you about the gods of Egypt," he said.

He picked up a paintbrush, dipped it in black ink, and started writing hieroglyphs on the wall. The Great Magician kept writing and writing.

Finally, the Great Magician turned back around. "How many gods are there?"

Princess Shephara raised her hand. "More than one hundred."

"Correct," said the Great Magician.

Peter raised his hand.

"Go ahead," said the Great Magician.

"I believe there is only one true God," said Peter.

He felt the leather bag shake under the table.

"You sound like those Israelite slaves with their weak God," said the Great Magician.

Peter stood and put his hands on his hips. "God is strong! He is not weak."

The Great Magician scoffed at Peter. "If your God is so strong, why are they still slaves?"

"Maybe God is waiting for the right time," said Peter.

The Great Magician's eyes filled with anger.

"That's enough from you," he said. "Now, back to my lesson . . . before you confuse the princess." He turned and continued writing hieroglyphs on the wall.

Mary raised her hand.

"What is your question?"

Mary pointed at a flag symbol at the beginning of each name. "Why is there a flag in front of every name?"

"That symbol means *god*," said the Great Magician.

Mary grabbed Peter's arm. "We will be back in a few minutes."

"Don't be long," said the Great Magician. "You two have a lot to learn."

Peter grabbed the bag and followed Mary and Hank into the hallway.

"Didn't that flag symbol look just like the one on the scroll?" said Mary.

"Yes! And I think the bag shook a minute ago." Peter eagerly pulled out the scroll and unrolled it. "It *is* the same flag!"

He held the scroll up in front of them. "Look!"

The scroll shook and the flag glowed and transformed into the word GOD. Then the hieroglyph beside it glowed and twisted into the word IS.

"We solved two words," said Mary.

They gave each other a high-five.

Hank growled. Peter heard footsteps coming down the hall. He shoved the scroll in the bag.

"What are you kids doing here?" said the Captain.

"We're on our way back to class," said Mary.

The Captain pushed them aside. "Class is canceled," he said. "Moses is back!"

The Great Magician threw down his paintbrush and grabbed his staff. "Moses is getting on my nerves!" He rushed out of the palace with the Captain.

"Let's go!" said Peter.

Peter, Mary, Hank, and Shephara ran to the river. They hid behind a small boat, out of view.

Moses and Aaron stood beside the Nile River. Pharaoh and the magicians walked down to meet them.

"God has a message for you," said Moses.

Pharaoh rolled his eyes. "What is it?"

"God says, 'Let my people go! If you refuse, I will bring a plague of frogs.'"

Pharaoh crossed his arms and shook his head.

Moses turned to Aaron and told him to hold his staff over the river. The blood-water bubbled

and gurgled. Then frogs flooded out of the river. Thousands of frogs were hopping everywhere.

Hank chased them. A slimy frog hopped on Shephara's head. She screamed and ran in circles.

The Great Magician clapped his hands. "Nice trick, but I can do it too."

There was a large fountain beside the palace. The Great Magician mumbled some mysterious words and waved his staff over the fountain.

Everyone waited and waited. Then two tiny tree frogs hopped out of the fountain.

"Not very impressive," said Mary.

"It looks like God is more powerful," said Peter.

The leather bag started shaking. Peter motioned to Mary, and they ran behind a palm tree, with Hank right behind them. Peter pulled out the scroll and unrolled it. The third hieroglyph glowed and transformed into the word POWERFUL.

"We solved the first three words," said Peter. "GOD IS POWERFUL."

A slimy frog hopped on top of the scroll.

"These frogs are freaking me out!" said Peter.

8

THE ROYAL DAGGER

The next few days were terrible. The Nile was still filled with blood, so drinking water was hard to find. The only way to get water was to dig in the mud next to the river and find water underground.

Peter looked out the window. He felt bad for the slaves who had to work all day just to find enough water for Pharaoh, the magicians, and Shephara. Plus, it smelled so bad!

Then there were the frogs! They really got on Peter's nerves. They jumped all over everything— on his head, in his food, and even on his bed.

The blood and frogs were just the beginning of the terrible things that had happened. Peter opened the adventure journal and read what he had written over the last several days.

Day 4
Pharaoh was sick of the frogs. He told Moses he would let the Israelite slaves go if Moses would ask God to take the frogs away. Moses prayed, and all the frogs died. Now there are piles of dead frogs everywhere. Then Pharaoh changed his mind and didn't let the slaves go free. You can't trust Pharaoh.

Day 5
Moses and Aaron came back to the palace after Pharaoh backed out of his deal. Aaron hit the ground with

his staff, and the dirt turned into annoying, gross little gnats. The Great

Magician tried to do it too, but he couldn't. He kept hitting the ground with his staff, but nothing happened. He was so mad that he finally ran off, away from the palace.

Day 6

I thought the gnats were bad, but then this happened. Moses and Aaron showed up and asked Pharaoh to let the Israelites go free. He said no again. That guy is so stubborn. Moses held his staff in the air. Then we were surrounded by a swarm of flies.

Nasty, dirty flies were everywhere. Princess Shephara ran around waving her arms in the air. All this buzzing is getting on my nerves.

Peter turned to a new page in the journal. A lot had happened that day too. After the flies were gone, Pharaoh had changed his mind again. The next plague was the worst yet. The Egyptians' animals got sick and died—including Shephara's favorite camel. Peter remembered how upset she had looked when she found out. Peter wrote a new entry:

Day 7
Pharaoh made another promise to let the Israelites go. God took the flies

away, but Pharaoh broke his promise again. So an even worse plague came. The Egyptians' animals got sick and died.

Joseph told me that none of the Israelites' animals have died. God is protecting his people and their animals. Hank is okay. He didn't get sick. I am not sure how much worse it can get.

Peter closed the journal. He had a hard time falling asleep that night. The plagues were getting more and more difficult.

When Peter woke up the next morning, he jumped out of bed and started studying the scroll.

Mary walked over and looked over his shoulder.

Peter looked up at her. "We've got to solve this scroll and get out of Egypt."

Peter heard a knock on the door.

He quickly put the scroll and the journal in the bag. "Who is it?"

"It's Shephara."

Mary opened the door. Princess Shephara was a mess. Her eyes were red, and she looked like she hadn't slept in days.

"Moses and Aaron are back," she said.

"Maybe your dad will let the Israelites go this time," said Mary.

"I hope so," she said. "I don't think I can handle any more plagues."

Peter grabbed his bag and

they headed out. They hid behind some large flowerpots and watched as Pharaoh and the magicians walked out to meet Moses and Aaron.

"Where's the Great Magician?" asked Peter.

"No one has seen him since he ran away from the gnats a few days ago," said Princess Shephara. "I haven't had to go to school."

"Well at least one good thing happened to you," said Peter.

The bag shook. Mary gave Peter a look. He held it tight so Princess Shephara wouldn't notice.

Peter peeked around the flowerpots and saw Moses grab a handful of ashes out of a furnace. He threw them into the air. Peter watched as a strong gust of wind blasted the ashes everywhere.

The ashes landed on the Egyptians, and red, blistering boils popped up on their skin. Pharaoh and the magicians began scratching madly at the boils. They couldn't stop.

"Ouch!" shouted Princess Shephara. "My skin itches so bad!"

She ran out from behind the flowerpots to show her dad.

"Why don't you just let them go?" she pleaded.

The magicians agreed, but Pharaoh wouldn't listen. He wouldn't let the Israelites go free.

Moses and Aaron shook their heads and walked away.

Peter looked down at his arm. He didn't have any boils. He

looked at Mary, and she didn't have boils. Hank wasn't scratching either.

"Let's get out of here," said Mary.

They ran into the palace.

"Hold it right there!" shouted the Captain.

Peter, Mary, and Hank froze.

"Why were you hiding out there?" said the Captain, scratching furiously.

Peter slowly turned around and faced the Captain. "We were with Princess Shephara."

"I don't trust you three," said the Captain. He took a closer look at Peter. "Wait, why don't you have any boils?"

"God protected us," said Peter.

"You sound just like Moses," said the Captain. "Maybe you're spying for him."

"Well, it's been nice talking with you," said Peter. He slowly backed away. "I think we will be going now."

The bag shook.
Peter held it tight.

"What's in there?" asked the Captain. He grabbed it from Peter.

Peter tried to grab it back. But the Captain pulled out his sword, and Peter stepped back.

"Let's see what's inside," said the Captain.

"Princess Shephara!" shouted Peter. "We need your help!"

Princess Shephara came running. "What's wrong?"

"I think we have spies in the palace," said the Captain. He opened the bag and looked inside.

"We're not spies," said Peter.

"Well, maybe you're thieves," said the Captain. He pulled Great-Uncle Solomon's dagger out of the bag.

"It's the royal dagger!" The princess looked hurt and confused. She looked at Peter. "Why did you steal it?"

"Let's see what else is in the bag," said the Captain.

"Wait!" said Peter. "I can explain."

Mary gave Peter *the look* again, and he realized he couldn't explain.

Princess Shephara lowered her head. "Arrest them."

The Captain laid the bag on the ground and walked toward Peter and Mary.

"Hank!" said Peter. "Fetch!"

Hank ran between the Captain's legs and grabbed the bag.

The Captain spun around. "Give me that!" He reached for Hank.

"Time for a karate lesson," said Mary.

"Looks like an easy target," said Peter.

Mary ran straight at the Captain, who was still bending over. She jumped in the air and did a spinning kick right to his backside.

"*Oomph.*" The Captain fell flat on his face. The sword and the royal dagger slid across the floor.

"I don't think he'll be sitting down for a while," said Peter.

Mary ran over and picked up the dagger.

"Hank, run for the river," said Peter. "Don't let anyone take the bag."

Hank took off through the palace doors like a lightning bolt.

Princess Shephara just stood there with her mouth wide open.

Mary handed her the royal dagger. "This belongs to you."

"No," said Princess Shephara. "It belongs to royalty."

Mary winked at her. "Like I said. This belongs to you."

Princess Shephara hugged Mary tightly. "Thank you."

"Let's go! Now!" said Peter.

"Stop, thieves!" the Captain shouted from the floor.

9

THE GREAT SPHINX

"Guards!" shouted the Captain. "Get them!"

The royal guards came running from all over the palace, swords drawn.

"Run!" said Princess Shephara.

Mary and Peter darted out the palace doors and toward the river.

"Michael!" shouted Peter. "We could use a little help here!"

A flash of light flew over their heads.

Bang! The palace doors slammed shut. Peter looked back. Michael was standing with his wings spread wide, holding the doors closed.

"Get to the desert!" said Michael. "I'll take care of the guards!"

Peter grabbed the bag from Hank, and they ran beside the Nile River to the desert. Peter stopped and bent over to catch his breath.

"I think we're safe now," he said.

Mary sat under a palm tree, panting. "Let's get the scroll out and see why it was shaking."

The scroll shook again. Peter unrolled it and three of the hieroglyphic symbols glowed and transformed into the words: AND, WILL, and YOU.

Mary read, "GOD IS POWERFUL AND WILL _____ YOU _____."

"We only have two words left," said Peter. "What do we do now?"

"I guess we wait for Michael," said Mary.

The sun set behind the pyramids. Peter and

Mary drifted off to sleep under the star-filled desert sky.

~๑

The rising sun woke Peter. He was relieved that the guards hadn't found them.

Peter shook Mary's shoulder. "I'm tired of waiting," he said. "Let's explore."

Mary agreed. They climbed to the top of a sand dune. Mary took the binoculars out of the bag and looked across the desert.

"There's the Great Sphinx," said Mary. "We have to go see it."

They walked and walked. It was farther away than it looked. Suddenly, thick, dark clouds filled the sky. A few raindrops landed on Peter's head,

and lightning struck the desert sand. Then it started raining—hard.

"I hope we don't have another flood," said Peter.

Hank ran ahead. Peter and Mary walked faster toward the Great Sphinx.

Thud! Something hit the sand next to Peter. He picked up a ball of ice the size of a golf ball.

Thud! Thud! More slammed into the sand. Now they were the size of baseballs.

"It's hail! Run!" shouted Mary.

They dashed and darted and dodged the hail. They ran between the paws of the Great Sphinx and dove into the entrance. The hail pounded against the Sphinx, but they were safe.

"That was close," said Peter.

"I guess Pharaoh still won't let them go," said Mary.

"It looks like we're stuck here," said Peter.

"That's okay. Let's explore," said Mary.

Peter took out the flashlight, and they headed deep into the Sphinx. Peter saw some light coming from a room at the end of the hallway.

Hank barked and ran into the room. Peter and Mary ran in after him.

"Wow!" said Mary.

The large room glowed with flickering candles. Shelves filled with scrolls lined the walls.

"This must be an ancient library," said Mary.

Hank growled at something in the corner. Peter shined his flashlight toward it. Two glowing yellow eyes appeared in the shadows. The black panther crept into the light.

"Not you again," said Peter.

Hank growled at the big cat. Peter and Mary stood back-to-back in the middle of the library as the black panther snarled and crept in a circle around them.

"Midnight, come here!" said a deep voice from a shadowy corner.

Peter turned his light that way. This time, the Great Magician's eyes glittered back at him.

"Well, look who decided to visit my little library," said the Great Magician.

The black panther sauntered over and curled up at his feet.

"I believe you've already met Midnight," said the Great Magician.

"How do you know?" said Mary.

"I know many things." The Great Magician walked over to a shelf and grabbed a scroll. "This scroll contains many secrets. Would you like to read it?"

"No, thanks," said Peter. He kept his eyes on the panther.

"How about you, Mary?" said the Great Magician.

Mary started to reach for the scroll. She loved secrets.

Peter grabbed her arm. "I think we should be going now," he said. "It sounds like the rain stopped."

"You just got here," said the Great Magician. "Stay. I have much to teach you." He pointed and Midnight ran to block the doorway. The panther showed its fangs and roared.

"I guess we can stay a little longer," said Peter nervously.

"I will make a deal with you," said the Great Magician. "I will let you go if you trade my scroll for the scroll in your bag."

"How did you know I had a scroll?" said Peter. He slowly pulled the scroll out of the bag and looked at it.

"I know a lot about you three," said the Great Magician. "We've met before."

"When?" said Mary.

"A long time ago," said the Great Magician. "We were in a garden." He pointed his snake-shaped staff at Mary. "You kicked me. And there was a great flood that you escaped somehow."

"We should have known it was you, Satan," said Mary.

Hank stepped in front of Mary and growled.

"Give me that scroll!" said the Great Magician.

Peter gripped the scroll tightly. "You'll never get it!"

"Do you children think you can stop my plan to crush God's people?" said the Great Magician.

"No," said Peter. "But God can!"

The Great Magician laughed. "Where is God?" he said. "You're all alone."

He swung his staff and knocked the scroll out

of Peter's grip. Midnight crouched low, ready to jump at them.

"We aren't alone," said Peter. "God is always with us."

Suddenly, a rushing wind blew through the room, extinguishing the candles.

A ball of light flew into the room and slammed into Midnight. The panther slid across the floor and knocked over a shelf. Hundreds of scrolls rolled across the floor.

"Oh no!" said Mary. "Which one is ours?"

The ball of light transformed into Michael.

"It's too late," said the Great Magician. "Pharaoh will never let God's people go!"

"It's never too late

for God!" said Michael. He drew his flaming sword and swung.

Peter and Mary got on their hands and knees and searched for the scroll.

"I can't find it!" said Mary.

Peter looked over his shoulder. He saw a blur of black fur, fangs, purple, and light. Candle stands and shelves crashed to the floor.

"More scrolls," said Mary. "We're never going to find it."

Hank dug through the scrolls and barked.

Peter ran across the library, ducking under Michael's swinging sword. He found Hank with a scroll in his mouth. It had the red wax seal.

"Hank found it!" shouted Peter.

Everyone froze.

"Run!" shouted Michael. "I will find you."

"Unless I find them first," said the Great Magician.

10

A City in the Sun

Peter, Mary, and Hank ran out of the Great Sphinx and didn't look back. Breathing hard, Mary motioned to Peter to stop under a palm tree.

"I hope Michael is okay," she said.

"I'm sure he's fine," said Peter. "He is the leader of God's angel army."

"What do we do now?" said Mary.

"We wait for Michael to find us," said Peter.

They waited and waited, but he didn't come. The sun set behind the pyramids, and Peter and Mary fell asleep under the palm tree.

Peter woke to the bright sun and a strong wind blowing in from the east. Hank ran to the top of a sand dune and barked.

Peter climbed to the top too. "Mary, look."

"What is it?" said Mary.

"I don't know," said Peter. "It looks like the sand is moving this way."

Mary looked through the binoculars. "That's not sand," she said. "It's bugs! It's locusts!"

The swarm of locusts moved closer.

"Hurry," said Mary. "Give me a boost."

Mary scrambled up the tree, and Peter lifted Hank up to her. The buzzing and chirping of the locusts grew louder.

"Hurry!" said Mary. "They're almost here!"

Peter grabbed onto the tree and climbed to the top. The locusts covered the desert below.

Mary ducked and shrieked. "Help!"

Michael swooped over their heads. He flapped his mighty wings and cleared a spot in the sand.

"Jump!" shouted Michael.

They jumped out of the tree.

"Duck!" said Michael. He covered them with his wings.

Peter heard the locusts marching over them as they huddled under Michael's wings. The buzzing finally stopped, and Michael stood up.

Peter looked at what was left of the tree. "Those were some hungry bugs," he said.

"You need to go to Goshen," said Michael. "You will be safe there."

"Where's Goshen?" said Mary.

"Didn't you pack a map?" said Peter.

Mary unrolled the map. "It's in Egypt. On the other side of the pyramids from Pharaoh's palace."

"You better get going," said Michael. "It's not safe here. I have to find the Great Magician."

Michael spread his wings and was gone.

"Let's go," Peter said.

Mary studied the map and looked out through the binoculars. "Follow me."

They walked and walked across the dry desert.

"Are you sure we're not lost?" said Peter

Mary looked at the map again. "I'm sure." She pointed. "Look, pyramids."

A strong wind blew from the west. Peter heard the buzzing sound again. "The locusts are coming back!"

Peter, Mary, and Hank ran to the pyramids. The wind blew harder and the buzzing grew louder. They found a small entrance and wriggled in. The swarm of locusts flew past them.

Darkness filled the pyramid. "It seems a little early for it to get so dark," said Peter.

"I guess we will have to stay here tonight," said Mary.

～❂

Peter stretched and rubbed his eyes. It should have been morning, but it was completely dark outside.

"Mary! Hank! Where are you?"

"I'm right here," said Mary. She reached out and touched his shoulder.

"Am I blind?" said Peter.

"No," said Mary. "It's just really dark."

"The darkness is so thick I can almost feel it," said Peter. "How will we find our way to Goshen?"

"Try your flashlight," said Mary.

Peter turned on the flashlight, but it didn't help much. They stumbled out of the pyramid into the darkness. Peter was glad there weren't many things to trip over in the desert.

They walked and walked and walked.

"How long have we been walking?" asked Peter.

"A long time," said Mary. "I don't even know where we are!"

Hank barked, and Peter saw a small light appear in the distance. "I hope it's not the Great Magician."

The light grew brighter. It was Michael's flaming sword!

"There you are," said Michael. "It was hard to find you in this darkness."

Mary shielded her eyes from the bright sword. "I think we got lost."

"I don't even know what day it is," said Peter. He pulled out the scroll and unrolled it. "How many days do we have left to solve the scroll?"

Michael counted on his fingers. "This is the your eleventh day in Egypt. You have today and three more days."

"We only have two words left," said Peter. "I think we can do it."

Mary looked at the map. "How are we going to find Goshen?"

"Follow me," said Michael.

Michael's flaming sword led the way up a tall sand dune. When they reached the top, they saw a city bathed in daylight.

Michael spread his arms. "Welcome to Goshen."

"Wow!" said Peter. "God even protects his people from the darkness."

"You'll be safe here," said Michael.

"Where do we go?" said Mary.

"When you enter the gate, take your first right turn," said Michael. "Then go to the third house on the right."

"What do we say?"

"Tell them God sent you," said Michael. He spread his wings and flew off into the darkness.

They found the house and knocked on the door. An older lady with a kind face opened the door.

"Hello. God sent us," said Mary.

"Oh, dear," said the lady. "Come in."

"Thank you," said Peter.

"Let me tell my husband you are here," she said. "Moses, we have visitors!"

11

ONE MORE PLAGUE

"Welcome to my home," said Moses. "This is my wife, Zipporah."

"Pleased to meet you," said Peter.

"You look familiar," said Moses. "Did I see you at Pharaoh's palace?"

"Yes," said Peter. "It's a long story."

"I love stories," said Zipporah. "Please tell us."

Peter told them how they were rescued by Pharaoh's daughter out of the Nile River. How they lived in the palace like Egyptian royalty. How things started getting difficult, with the plagues.

How they were accused of being criminals and had to escape into the desert. "I know it sounds like a crazy story," said Peter. "But it's true."

Moses smiled. "I believe you," he said. "We have a lot in common."

"You must be exhausted," said Zipporah. "Please, rest."

Peter and Mary plopped down on the cushions. Hank curled up at Peter's feet.

"You escaped the palace just in time," said Moses. "It's about to get even worse."

Mary sat up straight. "How could things get worse?"

"God is bringing one more plague," said Moses. "Then Pharaoh will let Israel go."

"What's going to happen?" said Mary.

"At midnight, all of the firstborn sons in Egypt will die," said Moses.

A chill ran through Peter's body. "I'm a

firstborn son," he said. His eyes widened. "Am I going to die?"

"No," said Moses. "You're safe here."

"Are you sure?" said Peter.

"Yes," said Moses. "Let me show you why you are safe."

Peter, Mary, and Hank followed Moses outside. He pointed to a lamb lying dead on a small table. "This lamb will protect you."

How is a dead lamb going to save my life? Peter's heart pounded.

Moses picked up a small bowl filled with blood from the lamb. "God told us to take blood from a perfect lamb and paint it on the top and side doorposts."

The sun began to set. "It's time," said

Moses. He picked up a small branch covered in leaves. He dipped it in the blood and marked the doorposts.

"Are you sure that's enough?" said Peter. After all, his life was at stake.

"Yes," said Moses. "This is exactly what God told me to do." Moses pointed at the dark sky. "Death will pass over—or skip—every house protected by the blood of the lamb."

Peter looked out and saw two young men coming down the road. They ran up and hugged Moses.

"These are my sons, Gershom and Eliezer," said Moses.

"Why did you want us to come?" asked Gershom.

"It sounded important," said Eliezer.

"The time has come," said Moses. "The time to be free."

Peter was not interested in talking. He was worried about dying.

"Which one of you is the oldest?" he said to Moses' sons.

"I am," said Gershom.

"Well, you better get inside," said Peter. He grabbed Gershom's arm and pulled him through the door.

Moses carried the lamb and gave it to Zipporah. She started a fire in the brick oven and cooked the lamb. Later, they ate the lamb and waited for death to pass over.

A strong wind howled outside, but Hank didn't make a sound.

Peter's heart thumped. "I hope this works."

"Trust God," said Mary.

"Easy for you to say," said Peter. "You're a girl. We should have solved the scroll earlier so we could be out of here."

The rushing wind stopped.

Peter looked out the window. It was calm. Then he heard shouts of joy coming from the houses of the Israelites. They were alive. Death had passed over them.

Then Peter heard cries of sorrow from the Egyptian houses across the desert. Death did not pass over them.

There was a knock at the door. It was the Captain.

"Pharaoh wants to see you," he said to Moses. He turned and walked away with his head lowered.

"It's time to go," said Moses.

Everyone followed Moses. As they left Goshen and headed to Pharaoh's palace, Peter looked back. There were Israelites as far as he could see.

"There must be a million people," said Mary.

Pharaoh stood at the palace entrance. Peter could tell his hard heart was broken.

"Get out of Egypt!" said Pharaoh. "And take the rest of the Israelites with you."

Joseph and his little sister ran out of the palace. "I'm free!" he shouted. "I'm finally free!"

"Peter! Mary!" shouted a girl's voice. "Wait!"

Princess Shephara caught up to them. Tears rolled down her cheeks.

"My brother died," she said.

Mary hugged her. "I'm sorry."

Princess Shephara wiped the tears from her

eyes. "I must be brave," she said. "I will be queen someday."

Peter looked ahead. The Israelites were leaving Egypt.

"Before you go," she said, "I have gifts for you."

She gave Mary a golden necklace with a brilliant blue amulet. She gave Hank a silver collar with a red ruby.

"I'm sorry, but we have to go now," said Peter.

"Wait, this is for you," said Princess Shephara. She handed him a golden staff. It had a cobra's head with red ruby eyes. "Now go. I must comfort my people." A tear rolled down her cheek.

"You will be a good queen," said Mary.

"Goodbye, Princess . . . I mean, *Queen* Shephara," said Peter. He bowed quickly and turned to leave.

Peter, Mary, and Hank joined the Israelites as they left Egypt—free at last.

They ran to the front to be closer to Moses. As they approached the desert, Peter saw a huge pillar of fire stretching into the night sky. The pillar of fire moved ahead of them. God was leading the way!

They walked the rest of the night. And when the sun rose, the Israelites followed a pillar of cloud. They walked all day and again all night.

Finally, the next day, they stopped at the Red Sea. Peter looked around. The sea was too deep and wide to cross. So the group set up camp and rested.

Hank barked and ran out of the camp. Peter and Mary chased him. When Hank finally stopped, he growled at something in the distance.

Peter looked through the binoculars. The Great Magician and Midnight were standing on top of a sand dune.

"This can't be good!" said Peter.

12

THE FINAL BATTLE

The Great Magician and Midnight turned and disappeared behind the sand dune.

"Let's see where they're going," said Peter.

They climbed to the top and saw a chariot speeding away, across the desert to Pharaoh's palace.

"He just won't give up," said Peter.

"Let's go," said Mary.

Back at camp, Peter pulled out the journal and wrote:

Day 13

I haven't written in a few days. Things have been pretty hectic, and now we only have one day left to solve the secret of the scroll. The Israelites are finally free! God showed Pharaoh how powerful he is. But I am a little worried about what the Great Magician has up his sleeve.

Peter put the journal away and laid his head on the leather bag. He stared up at the glittering sky and drifted off to sleep.

The sun rose and the Israelites prepared to keep going, but the pillar of cloud didn't move. So everyone waited.

After a while, Peter felt the ground rumbling.

It was barely noticeable at first. "Mary, do you feel that?"

"Yes," said Mary. "I hope it's not another plague."

The rumbling got stronger.

"I hope it's not an earthquake," said Peter.

Peter walked to the edge of camp. Mary came up behind him and looked through the binoculars. She groaned. "It's not an earthquake." She handed the binoculars to Peter.

He looked out across the desert. Hundreds of chariots and soldiers were coming their way. The sun reflected off their suits of armor, and a cloud

of sand came from the pounding hooves of the horses. Thousands of soldiers marched behind the chariots, while Pharaoh led the charge.

Peter turned the other way and saw the Red Sea. "We're trapped!"

They ran back to the Israelite camp. Everyone was panicking—except for Moses. He climbed up the side of a desert mountain to talk to the people.

"Did you lead us into the desert just to die?" shouted one man.

"I wish we had stayed in Egypt as slaves," a woman wailed.

Moses quieted the crowd and said, "Don't be afraid. Stand still and watch God rescue you today!"

The Israelites looked across the desert and saw the Egyptian army marching closer.

"This will be the last time you see the Egyptians," said Moses. "God will fight for you!"

The pillar of cloud moved between the Israelites and the Egyptian army.

"Halt!" shouted the Captain. The army did not pass the pillar. The Israelites stood their ground.

As the sun set, Moses held up his arms and stretched his staff over the Red Sea. God made a strong wind blow from the east. It blew harder and harder, until it made the water split right down the middle.

The wind kept blowing. It held the tall walls of water in place. The Israelites walked across

the dry ground in the middle. Peter, Mary, and
Hank followed them into the bed of the Red Sea.
The walls of water stood high above their heads.
As Peter walked, he saw a school of fish swim by.

"This reminds me of the aquarium," said
Peter. He stuck his hand into the water.

"Get your hand out!" said Mary. "You don't
know what's in there."

Just then, a shark swam by. Peter stumbled
back and rolled across the ground. Hank growled
at the shark, and it swam away. Peter brushed

himself off and picked up his bag and the golden staff.

"Let's catch up with the Israelites," said Mary. "They're almost across."

They jogged to the edge of the Red Sea and finally crossed onto the shore.

Mary said, "Let's look at the scroll again. We have to solve it before the sun rises, or we'll be stuck here!"

Peter reached down to pull out the scroll. His heart raced—the bag was unzipped. He searched the bag. "It's gone!"

"Where is it?" said Mary.

"I don't know," said Peter. "It must have fallen out when I dropped the bag."

They hurried back into the Red Sea to look for it.

"There it is!" said Peter. It was on the sea floor, not far away. Peter felt the ground rumbling. He looked up and saw the Great Magician riding a chariot toward the scroll. Peter sprinted toward it, but the horse was too fast.

The Great Magician leaned out of the chariot and scooped up the scroll. "Looking for this?" he said with an evil grin.

"Give it back!" shouted Peter.

"The scroll is mine!" shouted the Great Magician. "Have fun fighting the Egyptian Army." The chariot began to speed away.

Just then, Peter saw a glowing ball in the water. It grew bigger and burst through the wall of water. It flew into the chariot and knocked the wheels off. The

ball of light became Michael. He drew his flaming sword and knocked the Great Magician out of the chariot. The scroll flew out of his hand.

Mary ran to pick it up, but Midnight leaped in front of her and roared. She backed away. Michael charged into the panther and sent him rolling into the sea.

The Great Magician picked up the scroll. Peter swung his golden staff like a baseball bat and hit the scroll out of his hand.

"Hank, fetch!"

Hank caught the scroll mid-air and brought it back to Peter.

The Great Magician huffed. "You can have your precious scroll for now. I don't need it."

"You're about to see the power of the Egyptian Army!" he snarled. "The Israelites will be destroyed."

"No, you're about to see the power of God!" said Peter. "He will set them *free!*"

The scroll shook in Peter's hand, and Mary ran to his side. He unrolled it and saw the last hieroglyphs glow and transform into the words: SET and FREE.

The wind stopped blowing and the walls of water became crashing waves. The waves swallowed the Egyptian Army, and they were rushing toward the Great Magician, Peter, Mary, and Hank.

The Great Magician made one last attempt to grab the scroll as the sea swirled around them.

Peter held up the scroll and read, "GOD IS POWERFUL AND WILL SET YOU FREE!"

Then the water was gone. Peter, Mary, and Hank stood safe and dry in Great-Uncle Solomon's library. The red wax seal transformed into a gold medallion inscribed with a pyramid.

"That was way too close," said Peter.

Great-Uncle Solomon rushed into the library. "Welcome back!" he said. "You three look like Egyptian royalty." He laughed. "I like your skirt, Peter."

"It's not a skirt," said Peter.

"We had an amazing adventure," said Mary. She told Great-Uncle Solomon about the pyramids and the palace and the Great Sphinx.

"It sounds exciting," said Great-Uncle Solomon.

"It wasn't all fun," said Peter. He told him about the frogs and flies and the hailstorm. He told him how the Great Magician tried to take the scroll. Peter also told Great-Uncle Solomon about the lambs that were sacrificed to save his life and the lives of the other firstborn sons. He ended his story. "God showed his power and set the Israelites free."

Great-Uncle Solomon grabbed his big red Bible from a bookshelf. "Let me tell you the rest of the story." He told them how God led the Israelites through the desert for forty years. He told them God protected the Israelites and gave them all of the food and water they needed. Then he told them how the people stopped trusting God and started complaining about everything. "Because of this, most of them never got to go into the Promised Land."

"What's the Promised Land?" said Peter.

"That's a story for another day," said Great-Uncle Solomon. He also told them how God would send another sacrifice that was better than the lamb—a sacrifice that would save the world.

"I can't wait to find out what happens," said Mary.

Peter smiled and wondered where the scrolls would take them next.

*Do you want to read more
about the events in this story?*

The people, places, and events in *The Great Escape* are drawn from the stories in the Bible. You can read more about them in the following passages of the Bible.

Exodus chapters 1 and 2 tell the story of Egypt's oppression of Israel, the birth of Moses, and the Israelites' cry to God for help.

Exodus chapters 3 and 4 tell of God speaking to Moses from a burning bush and sending him to lead the people out of Egypt.

Exodus chapters 5–12 tell about Pharaoh's refusal to let the Israelites go and the ten plagues God sent to Egypt.

Exodus chapter 12 describes the first Passover and the Exodus from Egypt.

Exodus chapter 13 tells how God led the Israelites with a pillar of cloud and fire.

Exodus chapter 14 tells the story of the crossing of the Red Sea.

Special Notes:

1. Princess Shephara is a fictional character who represents the many daughters of pharaohs who would go on to become queens and pharaohs.

2. Events in *The Great Escape* have been condensed from the events presented in the book of Exodus.

CATCH ALL
PETER AND MARY'S
ADVENTURES!

In ***The Beginning***, Peter, Mary, and Hank witness the Creation of the earth while battling a sneaky snake.

In ***Race to the Ark***, the trio must rush to help Noah finish the ark before the coming flood.

In ***The Great Escape***, Peter, Mary, and Hank journey to Egypt and see the devastation of the plagues.

In ***Journey to Jericho***, the trio lands in Jericho as the Israelites prepare to enter the Promised Land.

In ***The Shepherd's Stone***, Peter, Mary, and Hank accompany David as he prepares to fight Goliath.

In ***The Lion's Roar***, the trio arrive in Babylon and uncover a plot to get Daniel thrown in the lions' den.

In ***The King Is Born***, Peter, Mary, and Hank visit Bethlehem at the time of Jesus' birth.

In ***Miracles by the Sea***, the trio meets Jesus and the disciples and witnesses amazing miracles.

In ***The Final Scroll***, Peter, Mary, and Hank travel back to Jerusalem and witness Jesus' crucifixion and resurrection.

ABOUT THE AUTHOR

 Mike Thomas grew up in Florida playing sports and riding his bike to the library and the arcade. He graduated from Liberty University, where he earned a bachelor's degree in Bible Studies.

When his son Peter was nine years old, Mike went searching for books that would teach Peter about the Bible in a fun and imaginative way. Finding none, he decided to write his own series. In The Secret of the Hidden Scrolls, Mike combines biblical accuracy with adventure, imagination, and characters who are dear to his heart. The main characters are named after Mike's son Peter, his niece Mary, and his dog, Hank.

Mike Thomas lives in Tennessee with his wife, Lori; two sons, Payton and Peter; and Hank.

For more information about the author and the series, visit www.secretofthehiddenscrolls.com.